Dear Parents and Educators,

Welcome to Penguin Young Readers! As parents and educators, you know that each child develops at his or her own pace—in terms of speech, critical thinking, and, of course, reading. Penguin Young Readers recognizes this fact. As a result, each Penguin Young Readers book is assigned a traditional easy-to-read level (1–4) as well as a Guided Reading Level (A–P). Both of these systems will help you choose the right book for your child. Please refer to the back of each book for specific leveling information. Penguin Young Readers features esteemed authors and illustrators, stories about favorite characters, fascinating nonfiction, and more!

Dick and Jane: Away We Go

LEVEL 1

GUIDED READING LEVEL **D**

This book is perfect for an **Emergent Reader** who:
- can read in a left-to-right and top-to-bottom progression;
- can recognize some beginning and ending letter sounds;
- can use picture clues to help tell the story; and
- can understand the basic plot and sequence of simple stories.

Here are some **activities** you can do during and after reading this book:
- Picture Clues: Use the pictures in this book to tell the story. Have the child go through the book, retelling the story by just looking at the pictures.
- Make Predictions: At the end of this story, Dick, Jane, and Sally see people riding in a yellow bus, in a red-and-yellow plane, and in a blue boat. Where do you think these people are going? Work with the child to write a paragraph that explains where you might go in a bus, where you might go in a plane, and where you might go in a boat.

Remember, sharing the love of reading with a child is the best gift you can give!

—Bonnie Bader, EdM
  Penguin Young Readers program

*Penguin Young Readers are leveled by independent reviewers applying the standards developed by Irene Fountas and Gay Su Pinnell in *Matching Books to Readers: Using Leveled Books in Guided Reading*, Heinemann, 1999.

PENGUIN YOUNG READERS
Published by the Penguin Group
Penguin Group (USA) LLC
375 Hudson Street
New York, New York 10014, USA

USA | Canada | UK | Ireland | Australia | New Zealand | India | South Africa | China

penguin.com
A Penguin Random House Company

Library of Congress Control Number: 2003016827

ISBN 978-0-448-43406-3   12

Dick and Jane
Away We Go

Penguin Young Readers
An Imprint of Penguin Group (USA) LLC

Contents

Chapter 1
Tim

Jump up, Sally.

Jump up.

Come, Sally.

Jump up.

Jump up, Tim.

Jump up.

Up, up, up.

Jump up.

Look, Dick.

See Sally and Tim.

Funny, funny Sally.

Funny, funny Tim.

Chapter 2
Tim and Spot

Go, Tim.

Go up.

Go up, Tim.

Go up, up, up.

Go, Tim.

Go down.

Go, go, go.

Go down.

Go down, down, down.

Oh, Jane.

See Spot and Tim.

See Spot run.

See funny Spot.

See funny Tim.

Chapter 3
Up, Tim

Up, Puff, up.

Come, Puff, come.

Oh, oh.

See Puff jump down.

Up, Puff, up.

Jump up, Puff.

Jump up.

See Tim.

Up, Tim, up.

Chapter 4

Run Away, Spot

"Oh, Spot," said Jane.

"You cannot play here."

Jane said,

"I can make a house."

"I can make a little house,"

said Jane.

"Down comes my house,"

said Jane.

"Down it comes.

Run away, Spot.

You cannot play here."

Chapter 5
Down It Comes

Dick said, "I can make a house.

A big house for two boats.

A house for the yellow boat.

And for the blue boat.

See my big house."

Jane said, "I can make a house.

A big house for three cars.

Red and blue and yellow cars."

Sally said, "I can make a house.

A little house for Tim.

Here is my house for Tim.

Tim is in it.

Tim can play in it.

Oh, oh, oh.

Tim looks funny in the house."

"See my house," said Dick.

"Down it comes."

"See my house," said Jane.

"Down, down it comes."

"Oh, oh, oh," said Sally.

"Down comes my little house.

Run away, Puff.

Run away, Spot.

You cannot play here."

Chapter 6
Away We Go

Sally said, "Away we go.

Away we go in the car.

Mother and Father.

Dick and Jane.

Sally and Tim."

Dick said, "Spot is not here.

Puff is not here."

Dick said, "I see something.

Look down, Jane.

Look down and see something.

It is funny.

Can you see it?"

"Oh, oh," said Jane.

"Here is Spot."

"Come in, Spot," said Jane.

"You can go in the car."

"Away we go," said Sally.

"Away we go in the car.

Mother and Father.

Dick and Jane.

Sally and Tim and Spot.

Away we go in the big, big car."

Chapter 7
See It Go

Jane said, "Look, look.

I see a big yellow car.

See the yellow car go."

Sally said, "I see it.

I see the big yellow car.

I want to go away in it.

I want to go away, away."

Dick said, "Look up, Sally.

You can see something.

It is red and yellow.

It can go up, up, up.

It can go away."

Sally said, "I want to go up.

I want to go up in it.

I want to go up, up, up.

I want to go up and away."

"Look, Sally," said Dick.

"Here is Father in a boat.

You can go away in it."

"Jump in, jump in," said Father.

"Jump in the big blue boat."

"We can go," said Sally.

"We can go away in the boat.

Away in a big blue boat."